Lessons Of Virtues Everyday

L.O.V.E

Cookies from love Mountain

By
Dea Walker

Ⓒ **Copyright**
Copyright License

There was a little girl named Jasper who lived in a far off village named Moosville. There village was known for having many cows and much milk. So one day Jasper was looking out at the evening sky and asked her mother "mommy the sky is so beautiful over by the mountains why don't we ever go there". Her mother looked at her and sighed "well Jasper honey we were told by the King that we are not allowed to venture up the mountain.

Jasper had a puzzled look on her face and wondered why they were not allowed to visit such a beautiful place. The next day came and Jasper decided to find out on her own why they weren't allowed to go to such a pretty place. She packed some water, food, a small blanket and one special item that she tucked away very carefully.

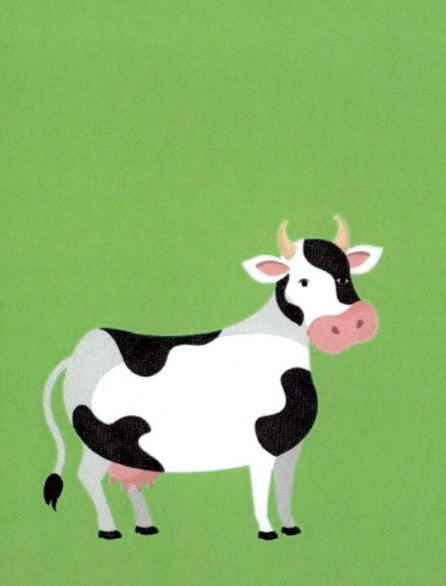

As she took off and ran through the meadows, she brushed her fingers through the flowers. The sky was becoming brilliant colors of red, orange, and yellow. Jasper said "well I better find a place to rest, night time will be here soon. She made it to the forest where she discovered an great willow tree and decided that it would make a perfect spot to sleep.

She opened her bag and pulled out her blanket and cuddled up under the huge tree. Creepy sounds crept in her ear and whistled through her hair but she stayed strong and thought of her mommy singing her a lullaby and before you know it she was fast asleep.

With her eyes still closed she could feel the warmth of the sun peeking though the branches of the tree. She heard the sounds of chirping, singing, and excitement in the air. She sprang up and shouted "its morning, time to get a move on". As she made her way through the forest to the base of the mountain she looked up to see the clouds mid way up. So she tighten her grip on her bag and started to make her journey up the mountain.

Finally, she made it to the point where the clouds took place on the mountain and with a few deep breaths she walked right threw them. The clouds tickled her cheeks and nose so much it made her laugh so hard she was crying with joy , she didn't even notice she was at the top of the mountain.

As she looked around she couldn't help but feel full of joy and very happy, not just because of the beauty of the mountain but something else that she couldn't quite put her finger on. She could see in the distance a town and decided to walk toward it. By her surprise a little boy came over to her and asked "hey was that you laughing out loud" Jasper nodded and smiled at the boy. "What's your name" she asked. The boy answered and said "Jacob". "I'm Jasper" she said, "I have traveled up here to find out why my village is not allowed to climb this mountain".

Jacob said "follow me I will take you to meet my mom, maybe she can help you". The two of them headed toward his home. Looking around the streets in the town everything looked so bright and shiny, even the people seemed to have a glow. Everyone was so friendly and happy that it made Jasper's heart feel like it was being tickled. They reached his house and he asked Jasper to stay at the door he will be right back.

Jasper seemed to have been waiting there for a long time that she started to think he had forgotten about her, when all of a sudden she noticed the door opening. It crept open slowly which made her feel a little scared but then it had a familiar smell. A very beautiful lady appeared with a plate of cookies "hi you must be Jasper I'm Belle, Jacobs mom pleased to meet you" Jasper smiled. Belle offered Jasper some cookies and as soon as she bit into the cookie she could only think of one thing.

So she took off he bookbag and pulled out that special item that she had tucked away ever so carefully. Jacob and his mom waited patiently as she unwrapped the item, "got it" She whispered. This was my granny's recipe, it's the same as the cookies you made, she would call them love cookies, but how can this be "they all shouted". Belle asked Jasper what's your granny's name "her name is Lilly" Jasper replied. Well that would make sense that was my moms best friend they would make these cookies for me as a little girl.

Jasper was excited to find out such good news but then she remembered she still didn't know why no one was allowed to climb the mountain so she asked Belle. Belle then started to tell the story of the great friendship between the two towns and how they would trade cookies for milk. until one day the king of Moosville became very bitter toward the village because his daughter fell in love with the mountain village. She decided to live up here, he begged her to stay to oversee the Moosville when it was time for her to rule but her heart did not want to rule, it wanted to be happy and free.

The day she left all trading was to stop and it was forbidden to climb the mountain. Jasper thought that was a very sad story and wanted to make a change. She came up with a great plan but she needed a little help. she asked Belle if she could make as many love cookies as possible and for Jacob to find the biggest wagon he could to stack the cookies on.

Jasper drew out her plan an explained it to the others, "first I will take the cookies down the mountain and then I will knock on the kings door and when he answers the door and speaks I will throw a love cookie in his mouth and when he swallows his heart will then shine with love and joy, our villages will be able to share and trade again.

Jacob thought the plan seemed good and he decided he would go and help her. He become fond of her and loved the idea of them becoming great friends. The two of them headed down the mountain and into the forest through the meadow and reached Moosville. The sun was setting soon so they rushed to he kings door and knocked but to their surprise the king didn't answer.

They looked at each other and wondered what they should do "I got it" Jacob said. He told Jasper to wait by the door and when the king comes out be ready. Jacob climbed a tree next to the kings window and jumped through it. the king spotted him and started to chase him all the way down the stairs to the front door and yelled "hey what are you doing".

Jasper threw a love cookie into his mouth and with a little hesitation he started to chew, his eyes seemed to light up and sparkle he began to smile "what a lovely cookie, may I have another" he said. The king asked "where did these cookies come from?" Jasper answered "the mountain". The king repeated what she said " the mountain, well we better start trading with them again".

Jasper and Jacob looked at each other and knew the plan worked. They went all around town and shared the love cookies and the cookies brought joy to everyone. Ever since that day the villages began to trade and make friends and find old friends. The king seen his daughter and they hugged each other and decided to never stay mad at each other again. Now both villages seemed to shine bright with love and joy. So remember to shine bright, forgive, spread love and joy.

Recipe for Love Cookies

1. Lots of love
2. 1 Stick of real butter
3. 1 1/4 Cup of organic brown sugar
4. 1 Teaspoon of pure vanilla extract
5. 2 Range free eggs
6. 1/2 Teaspoon of pink Himalayan salt
7. 2 Cups of organic flour
8. 1 Teaspoon of organic baking soda

Additional Ingredients

1 Cup of miniature peanut butter cups and 2 tbsp. of natural peanut butter

or

1 1/2 Cups organic oatmeal and 16 oz. of raisinets

or

1 Cup of organic chocolate chips

Just use your imagination and spread your own ingredients of love to your cookies!

About the author

Being a mom of five beautiful girls can sometimes be demanding and wonderful all at once. So when my girls were younger to keep us focused I put together a few good lessons by story telling. They enjoyed them so much I decided to write them down and create a collection of books to share. I hope to bring joy and love to all who reads them.

© **Copyright**
Copyright License

Made in the USA
Columbia, SC
25 July 2021